Perlorian™

Suzanne Green

Busy Day

DOUBLEDAY & COMPANY, INC.
GARDEN CITY, NEW YORK

TITLES IN THIS SERIES:

THE BIRTHDAY BOOK
BUSY DAY
GOING TO SCHOOL
SEASONS

Copyright © 1987 by Satoru Tsuda
All Rights Reserved
Printed in Italy
First Edition
Perlorian Cats is a trademark of Satoru Tsuda
Library of Congress Cataloging-in-Publication Data
Green, Suzanne.
Busy day.
Summary: Photographs depict young cat characters on
a busy day as they sweep the floor, wash the windows,
and perform other household tasks.
[1. Cats—Fiction. 2. House cleaning—Fiction]
I. Title.
PZ7.G82634Bu 1987   [E]   87-6843
ISBN 0-385-23507-0

Note to Grown-ups

The "Perlorian Cats" that you see here are very special animals photographed by a very caring group of photographers led by Satoru Tsuda. The cats are specially chosen for their expressive faces and comfort with the photography sessions.

These photographs are taken at incredibly high shutter speeds to capture a pose and an expression without any discomfort to the cat or cats involved. No artificial substances are used—just love and patience! And the cats seem to respond beautifully to the attention and caring that surround them.

Needless to say, no one should try to do this with cats or kittens on their own. Professional training and proper circumstances should always be involved when working with animals. Your family cat will not welcome treatment it is not used to. Cats are very independent animals!

I have nothing to wear on
cleaning day!

I am going to make
an apron.

I love to sew.

I wonder what my brothers
will wear.

I'd better finish this.

What do you think?

Don't I look perfect?

Mother is finally home from shopping.

What has happened here?!

Take off this apron . . .

and clean up this mess!

There is so much to do.

First we must sweep
the floor.

Then we must wash the windows.

As soon as we make lunch,
we can eat.

Boy, are we tired!

Your father would be proud of
how you worked. Now go play.

I wonder if Mouse wants
to play with us.

Come and play with us,
Mouse!

Isn't this fun?

We have to go to bed now.

It's been a busy day.

Mother reads us a story.

And it's off to sleep.